P9-CDO-998

THIEF OF THIEVES™

Date: 6/28/18

GRA 741.5 THI V.5
Diggle, Andy,
Thief of thieves. "Take me"

PALM BEACH COUNTY
LIBRARY SYSTEM
3650 Summit Boulevard
West Palm Beach, FL 33406-4198

CREATED BY ROBERT KIRKMAN

Andy Diggle
Writer

Shawn Martinbrough
Artist

Adriano Lucas
Colorist

Rus Wooton
Letterer

Sean Mackiewicz
Editor

Shawn Martinbrough
Adriano Lucas
Cover

THIEF OF THIEVES, VOL. 5: "TAKE ME."
ISBN: 978-1-63215-401-9
PRINTED IN U.S.A.
First Printing

Published by Image Comics, Inc. Office of publication: 2001 Center Street, 6th Floor, Berkeley, California 94704. Image and its logos are ® and © 2016 Image Comics Inc. All rights reserved. Originally published in single magazine form as THIEF OF THIEVES #26-31. THIEF OF THIEVES and all character likenesses are ™ and © 2016, Robert Kirkman, LLC. All rights reserved. All names, characters, events and locales in this publication are entirely fictional. Any resemblance to actual persons (living or dead), events or places, without satiric intent, is coincidental. No part of this publication may be reproduced or transmitted, in any form or by any means (except for short excerpts for review purposes) without the express written permission of the copyright holder.

For information regarding the CPSIA on this printed material call: 203-595-3636 and provide reference # RICH – 650085.

IMAGE COMICS, INC.
Robert Kirkman – Chief Operating Officer
Erik Larsen – Chief Financial Officer
Todd McFarlane – President
Marc Silvestri – Chief Executive Officer
Jim Valentino – Vice-President

Eric Stephenson – Publisher
Corey Murphy – Director of Sales
Jeff Boison – Director of Publishing Planning & Book Trade Sales
Jeremy Sullivan – Director of Digital Sales
Kat Salazar – Director of PR & Marketing
Emily Miller – Director of Operations
Branwyn Bigglestone – Senior Accounts Manager
Sarah Mello – Accounts Manager
Drew Gill – Art Director
Jonathan Chan – Production Manager
Meredith Wallace – Print Manager
Briah Skelly – Publicity Assistant
Sasha Head – Sales & Marketing Production Designer
Randy Okamura – Digital Production Designer
David Brothers – Branding Manager
Ally Power – Content Manager
Addison Duke – Production Artist
Vincent Kukua – Production Artist
Tricia Ramos – Production Artist
Jeff Stang – Direct Market Sales Representative
Emilio Bautista – Digital Sales Associate
Leanna Caunter – Accounting Assistant
Chloe Ramos-Peterson – Administrative Assistant
IMAGECOMICS.COM

For SKYBOUND ENTERTAINMENT

Robert Kirkman - CEO
David Alpert - President
Sean Mackiewicz - Editorial Director
Shawn Kirkham - Director of Business Development
Brian Huntington - Online Editorial Director
June Alian - Publicity Director
Rachel Skidmore - Director of Media Development
Jon Moisan - Editor
Arielle Basich - Assistant Editor
Dan Petersen - Operations Manager
Sarah Effinger - Office Manager
Nick Palmer - Operations Coordinator
Genevieve Jones - Production Coordinator
Andres Juarez - Graphic Designer
Stephan Murillo - Business Development Coordinator

International inquiries: foreign@skybound.com
Licensing inquiries: contact@skybound.com

WWW.SKYBOUND.COM

THREE MONTHS LATER.

I-- I CAN'T SLEEP. AND WHEN I DO, I'M BACK IN THAT TRUCK. OR THAT BASEMENT...
THAT'S ALL IN THE PAST NOW, HONEY. IT'S OVER.
THOSE PEOPLE CAN'T HURT YOU ANYMORE.
THAT'S BECAUSE-- BECAUSE WE KILLED THEM. I MEAN WE KILLED A LOT OF PEOPLE--
AUGUSTUS. LISTEN TO ME.
WE HAVE A FRESH START. YOU SHOULD BE THINKING ABOUT THE FUTURE NOW, NOT DWELLING ON THE PAST.

YEAH, THAT'S KIND OF WHAT I AM DOING.
LISTEN, I GOTTA GO.
AUG--?
BIP.

AUDREY! PLEASURE TO SEE YOU AGAIN.
ARE YOU LOOKING FOR THE SHIATSU OR SHALL WE TRY SOMETHING DIFFERENT TODAY...?
SURPRISE ME.
AND WHO KNOWS, MAYBE THERE'LL BE A SURPRISE IN IT FOR YOU, TOO...

MMMM.
NNNNGH.
GOD, THAT FEELS GOOD. DIDN'T KNOW HOW *TENSE* I WAS...
LET ME SEE WHAT I CAN DO ABOUT THAT. YOU ALWAYS SAID I WAS GOOD WITH MY *HANDS*...

CONRAD? WHAT THE FUCK ARE YOU DOING HERE?!
I-- GIVING YOU A MASSAGE...?
WHERE'S ZANE?
"ZANE?" IF YOU MEAN THE BEACH-BUM-SLASH-GYM-RAT, I JUST SLIPPED HIM A FIFTY.
LISTEN, I'M SORRY IF I STARTLED YOU. I JUST WANTED TO SURPRISE YOU...
NOT EVERYTHING IS ABOUT WHAT YOU WANT, CONRAD. YOU CAN'T JUST SNEAK INTO MY PRIVATE LIFE WHENEVER YOU--
OH, FORGET IT. WHAT'S THE POINT?

AUDREY, PLEASE. GIVE ME A CHANCE.
I DID WHAT YOU WANTED. I QUIT. I THINK I'M ENTITLED TO--
EXACTLY! THANK YOU, CONRAD, THAT'S EXACTLY THE WORD I WAS LOOKING FOR.
ENTITLED.
YOU THINK YOU'RE ENTITLED TO WHATEVER YOU WANT. AND IF SOMEONE SAYS YOU CAN'T HAVE IT, THAT JUST MAKES YOU MORE DETERMINED TO TAKE IT.
EVEN WHEN IT'S ME.
DAMMIT, AUDREY, WHAT DO I HAVE TO DO?
NOTHING. THERE IS NOTHING FOR YOU TO DO.
DON'T YOU GET IT? I'M NOT A FUCKING SAFE TO BE CRACKED. THERE IS NO MAGICAL COMBINATION THAT LETS YOU WIN ME BACK.
I'M NOT YOUR PRIZE, CONRAD.

... I'M SORRY, BUT I JUST-- I CAN'T DO THIS ANYMORE. HAVING THIS SAME CONVERSATION WITH YOU OVER AND OVER...
YOU HAVE TO LET ME GO.
... OKAY.
IF THAT'S WHAT YOU WANT.
IT IS. THANK YOU.
AND GOODBYE.

I-- I'LL LEAVE YOU ALONE.
I NEVER SAID I WANTED TO BE ALONE.
PLEASE SEND THE MASSEUR BACK IN.
YOU GET HER WARMED UP FOR ME?
DON'T WORRY, MAN, I'LL TAKE GOOD CARE OF HER.
REAL GOOD CARE...

804
FUCK!

GREAT. NO GLASSES. AND I BROUGHT *WHISKEY.*
... RELAX, TOUGH GUY. I'M NOT HERE TO THROW MYSELF AT YOU.
I NEVER MAKE THE SAME MISTAKE TWICE.
CELIA. WHAT ARE YOU--
NOPE, I THINK THE QUESTION YOU SHOULD BE ASKING YOURSELF IS, WHAT ARE *YOU* DOING HERE?
... FINALIZING MY DIVORCE.

GOOD. ONE LESS DISTRACTION, RIGHT?
ALTHOUGH I GOTTA SAY, YOU, UH... STILL LOOK PRETTY DISTRACTED.
SHE'S DOWNSTAIRS. FUCKING THE MASSEUR.
WHOAH, EASY, TIGER. YOU JUST SAID IT YOURSELF -- YOU'RE DIVORCED.
YOU DON'T GET TO POLICE AUDREY'S SEX LIFE.
... WHAT?

WAIT.
STOP.

LET'S DO THIS PROPERLY.

... ONE QUESTION.
DO YOU LOVE ME?
HA!
FUCK, NO.
GOOD.
SO YOU MIND TELLING ME WHY YOU'RE NOT IN ICELAND?
REALLY? YEARS OF UNFULFILLED SEXUAL TENSION RELEASED IN A BURST OF WORLD CHAMPIONSHIP-LEVEL WILD MONKEY SEX, AND THAT'S YOUR GO-TO LINE?

THIS WAS... PROBABLY A MISTAKE.
WOW, YOU KNOW JUST WHAT A LADY WANTS TO HEAR. I CAN'T IMAGINE WHY AUDREY LET YOU GO.
TOO SOON?

OKAY, YOU WANNA BE ALL BUSINESS? I CAN BE ALL BUSINESS.
SO I'VE BEEN HIDING OUT WITH DON PARRINO'S BLACKMAIL BOOK LIKE YOU ASKED...
MEANWHILE, EVERYONE IMPLICATED IN IT HAS BEEN MOVING THEIR MONEY TO UNTRACEABLE ACCOUNTS, COVERING THEIR TRACKS.
EVERY DAY WE WAIT, THE BOOK BECOMES LESS VALUABLE. WE SIT THIS OUT MUCH LONGER, IT'LL BE WORTH SHIT.
SO WHAT ARE YOU SUGGESTING?
WHAT ELSE? WE USE IT, MAN! MAKE HAY WHILE THE IRON'S HOT OR WHATEVER!
THE BOOK WAS MY BACKSTOP AGAINST PARRINO AND LOLA. THEY'RE DEAD.
IT'S SERVED ITS PURPOSE.
SO I GUESS I'VE SERVED MY PURPOSE TOO, HUH? LEFT TO FREEZE MY ASS OFF WHILE YOU STALK YOUR EX?
STARTING TO FEEL A LITTLE UNAPPRECIATED HERE, CONRAD. A LITTLE TAKEN FOR GRANTED.

CELIA--
NO, CONRAD! C'MON, IT'S TIME TO GET BACK IN THE GAME. YOU AND ME AGAINST THE WORLD, JUST LIKE OLD TIMES!
IT USED TO BE FUN, MAN. REMEMBER WHEN IT WAS FUN?
I MEAN YOU'RE REDMOND, FOR CHRISSAKES! THE WORLD'S GREATEST THIEF! THAT NAME MEANS SOMETHING TO PEOPLE IN OUR LINE OF WORK!
NOT ANYMORE.
I TOLD YOU A YEAR AGO. I QUIT.
BUT-- I THOUGHT... THAT WAS FOR AUDREY...
I MEAN, I'VE BEEN LINING UP SCORES. I GOT BUYERS WAITING...
NO.
I'M SORRY, BUT I'M DONE.
REDMOND IS DEAD.

AIRPORT.
BIP BIP BIP.
HELLO?

THIS IS REDMOND.

--THEY SAY LIGHTNING DOESN'T STRIKE TWICE; BUT APPARENTLY IT DID FOR ONE SAN DIEGO RESIDENT.
DEPARTMENT OF JUSTICE
FEDERAL BUREAU OF INVESTIGATION
FIDELITY BRAVERY INTEGRITY
FOX 5
SECURITY CONSULTANT CONRAD PAULSON IS SAID TO HAVE RECEIVED AN UNDISCLOSED SEVEN FIGURE SUM FOR HIS SECOND WRONGFUL ARREST AT THE HANDS OF THE FBI.
FOX 5
FEDERAL AGENT ELIZABETH COHEN, DESCRIBED AS A "ROGUE AGENT PURSUING A PERSONAL VENDETTA" BY SOURCES CLOSE TO THE CASE, WAS DISMISSED FROM THE BUREAU FOR HER ROLE IN BOTH ARRESTS.
FOX 5
MEANWHILE, THE NOTORIOUS MASTER THIEF KNOWN ONLY AS REDMOND, HIS TRUE IDENTITY STILL A MYSTERY, REMAINS AT LARGE--
BLAM!

NO.
YOU DON'T GET TO WIN.

... JESUS, LIZ.
CHK-CHAK!
SNIK!

SKRSSHH!
HOWARD

BUREAU OF SECURITY AND INVESTIGATIVE SERVICES.
YEAH, HI. I'D LIKE TO APPLY FOR A ***PRIVATE INVESTIGATOR'S LICENSE.***
AND IF THERE'S ANYTHING WE CAN DO TO SPEED THINGS ALONG, THAT'D BE GREAT...
I'M MAKING UP FOR LOST TIME HERE.

HEY, SIS.
OH. IT'S YOU.
YOU SHOULD HAVE CALLED AHEAD.
NICE TO SEE YOU, TOO, PENNY.
SO YOU GONNA MAKE ME STAND OUT HERE ALL DAY...?
"... OR CAN I SEE MY SON?"

HE LOOKS HAPPY.
HE IS. WE ARE.
YOU ALWAYS WERE BETTER AT THIS MOM SHIT. I GOT SKILLS, BUT MOTHERHOOD AIN'T ONE OF 'EM.
I BET YOU DO.
WHAT'S THAT SUPPOSED TO MEAN...?
WELL, I MEAN LOOK AT YOU! WITH YOUR TATTOOS AND YOUR PIERCINGS AND LORD KNOWS WHAT ELSE. WHAT ARE PEOPLE SUPPOSED TO THINK?
FUCK'S SAKE, PENNY! WHAT DO YOU THINK, I'M TURNING TRICKS AT THE BUS DEPOT OR SOMETHING?

I DON'T KNOW, ARE YOU? I MEAN, DO YOU EVEN KNOW WHO LEROY'S FATHER IS?
YOU LEAVE HIM HERE AND RUN OFF TO WHO-KNOWS-WHERE FOR MONTHS AT A TIME--
I'M TRYING TO BUILD A FUTURE FOR HIM, OKAY? GIVE HIM WHAT WE NEVER HAD.
YOU DON'T KNOW WHAT IT WAS LIKE. I HAD TO PROVIDE FOR ALL OF US WHILE YOU WERE LOOKING AFTER MOM. SHE HAD NOTHING.
WE HAVE NOTHING. WE GET BY.
YOU NEED SOME CASH? JUST SAY THE--
NO! I DO NOT WANT YOUR DIRTY MONEY.

MOM!
HEY, LITTLE TIGER! HOW YOU BEEN?
ARE YOU HERE TO STAY THIS TIME?
SOON, KIDDO. REAL SOON.
I JUST GOT ONE OR TWO MORE THINGS TO DO FIRST. AND THEN WE'RE GOOD.

HOME SWEET HOME.
QUITE THE BACHELOR PAD...
... AND SO DELIGHTFULLY UNDERSTATED.
IT'S AN INVESTMENT, FOXLEY.
ALL THIS MONEY, WHAT ELSE AM I SUPPOSED TO DO WITH IT? PUT IT IN A BANK, HIGH-RISK STOCKS?
YOU CAN'T STEAL A HOUSE.

SPEAKING OF MONEY...
MERRY CHRISTMAS. COURTESY OF THE FBI.
THE NEW SETTLEMENT? CHRIST, WHAT AM I SUPPOSED TO DO WITH THIS...?
YOU'RE WELCOME. NOT LEAST FOR MY PERCENTAGE. AND TO THINK, MOTHER WAS SO DISAPPOINTED WHEN I CHOSE LAW OVER THE CLERGY...
SO WHAT'S NEXT?
NEXT?
YOU'RE FOOTLOOSE AND FANCY-FREE! AS FAR AS THE FBI IS CONCERNED, YOU'RE RADIOACTIVE. THEY WON'T DARE COME WITHIN A MILE OF YOU.
YOU COULD SELFIE YOURSELF RIPPING OFF FORT KNOX AND THEY'D FALL OVER THEMSELVES CLAIMING YOU HAD NOTHING TO DO WITH IT!
CONRAD

YOU'RE IN A RUT, DEAR BOY, AND SPEAKING BOTH AS YOUR PERSONAL FRIEND AND YOUR LEGAL COUNSEL, I WOULD WHOLEHEARTEDLY ENCOURAGE YOU TO SEIZE THIS OPPORTUNITY TO ENGAGE IN SOME HIGH-END GRAND LARCENY.
SO WHAT'S NEXT?
I'M RETIRED.
WHAT?
JUST WAITING FOR THE PUNCHLINE.
YOU DON'T THINK I'M SERIOUS?
I GIVE IT A WEEK. YOU'LL BE CLIMBING THE WALLS.
LITERALLY.

UNTIL THEN, I SUPPOSE YOU COULD ALWAYS OCCUPY YOURSELF WITH A SPOT OF UNPACKING...
WHAT'S THE POINT? IT'S JUST... STUFF.
I DON'T NEED STUFF.
SO WHAT DO YOU NEED?
I NEED ANOTHER DRINK.

GHOSTS OF CAPERS PAST.
A GOOD CREW'S A TERRIBLE THING TO WASTE.
REDMOND'S BACK IN BUSINESS. YOU GAME?
I HEARD CONRAD QUIT.
HE DID. I'M REDMOND NOW.
SHIT, GIRL. HE COOL WITH THAT?
FORGET CONRAD. HE HAD A GOOD THING AND HE THREW IT AWAY. LET HIM STEW IN HIS BOOZE, IF HE WANTS.
I'M STEPPING UP.

AFTER THE VENICE JOB. I BOUGHT HORSES. HELL, I BOUGHT THE *TRACK.*
WHY RISK IT ALL? IT'S NOT LIKE WE NEED THE MONEY...
SPEAK FOR YOURSELF. MY CUT CAME OUT OF CONRAD'S, AND HE REFUSED TO GO THROUGH A FENCE.
SAY WHAT?
HE HAD A CUT-OUT RETURN HIS SHARE OF THE ART TO ITS ORIGINAL OWNERS. REWARD FEE'S A *FRACTION* OF WHAT HE'D HAVE MADE ON THE BLACK MARKET.
DAMN. SO HE REALLY DID IT. SON OF A BITCH TURNED INTO AN HONEST CITIZEN.
HE CAN AFFORD TO.

THEY ALL SAID NO?
EVERY ONE OF 'EM. TOO COMFORTABLE.
NO ONE EVER DIED FROM BEING TOO COMFORTABLE.
DON'T YOU BELIEVE IT.
SO WHAT'S THE SCORE?
INDUSTRIAL DESIGN. DEFENSE CONTRACTOR FIGURES THEY CAN BUILD A FUSION REACTOR THAT FITS ON THE BACK OF A TRUCK.
BUYER REACHED OUT TO REDMOND ON THE DARK WEB. I'M GUESSING SOME OIL COMPANY EXEC WORRIED ABOUT HIS LONG-TERM BOTTOM LINE.

YOU WANT TO STEER CLEAR OF THAT UNDERNET CRAP, HONEY. NEVER KNOW WHO YOU'RE REALLY DEALING WITH.
YOU WORK WITH THE PEOPLE YOU KNOW.
YOU TRUST THE PEOPLE YOU KNOW?
NO. BUT YOU KNOW WHO TO HIT, THEY FUCK YOU OVER.
OR IF THEY GET CAUGHT AND COP A PLEA BARGAIN.
... IS THAT A *THREAT?*
JUST A NOTE OF CAUTION, HONEY.
YOU'RE WELL-LIKED. BUT YOU KNOW THAT DOESN'T MEAN SHIT.

SO MUCH FOR BRAND LOYALTY.
... FUCK 'EM.

TAK TAK TAK.
KeyStrokeLog:
ZZ9pluralZalpha
YES!

NOPE.

DON'T SUPPOSE I COULD INTEREST EITHER OF YOU GENTS IN A MILLION DOLLARS?
THAT'S RIGHT, HONEY. ADD ATTEMPTED BRIBERY OF A POLICE OFFICER TO THE LIST. THAT'S ANOTHER COUPLE YEARS RIGHT THERE.
NOT THAT IT'LL MAKE MUCH DIFFERENCE. TIME YOU GET OUT, WE'LL BE LIVIN' ON MARS OR SOME SHIT.
ELEVATORS ARE ON LOCKDOWN. GOTTA TAKE THE STAIRS.
TERRIFIC, NOW THIS...

SNIK
GOTTA SAY, I'M A LITTLE DISAPPOINTED. FIGURED THE FAMOUS REDMOND'D BE EASIER TO--
WUHH--!

DON'T--
UHHF!
THAPP
SNAK

FUCKING
BITCH!
BLAM
PANNGG

NO--!
OOF!
BLAM
BLAM
BLAM
BLAM
BLAM

EMERGENCY EXIT
UNGHH!
MOTHER.
FUCKER.

... WHO THE HELL ARE YOU?

YOU'RE NO COP.
THAT IS CORRECT. I'M SPECIAL AGENT NATHAN DOUGLAS, FBI. AND YOU ARE...?
PISSED.
CLAIMING THE FIFTH. AS IS YOUR RIGHT.
NO NAME GIVEN. NO I.D. AT TIME OF ARREST. THAT'S OKAY...
WE'LL JUST CALL YOU *REDMOND.*

I TAKE IT YOU'VE BEEN READ YOUR MIRANDA RIGHTS...?
THIS IS BULLSHIT. SINCE WHEN IS PETTY LARCENY A FEDERAL CRIME?
GRAND LARCENY. ATTEMPTED. AND SINCE THE COMPANY YOU BURGLARIZED WAS A GOVERNMENT DEFENSE CONTRACTOR...
WELL. YOU CAN SEE WHERE THIS IS GOING.
I SHOULD WARN YOU THAT REFUSAL TO IDENTIFY YOURSELF TO A FEDERAL AGENT MAY BE ARGUED IN COURT AS OBSTRUCTION OF JUSTICE, COMPOUNDING YOUR GUILT AND INCREASING YOUR SENTENCE.
SO WHAT'S YOUR NAME, SWEETHEART?
MIRANDA.

SIR?
SIR...?
SIR, IF YOU DON'T MIND, WE HAVE A GROUP COMING THROUGH HERE.
... SORRY. I WAS MILES AWAY. PLEASE.
AN *EMPTY FRAME?* FOR *THIS* WE PAY FOR A GALLERY TOUR...?
IT'S *MODERN ART,* HONEY.
WELL, YES AND NO. THIS IS WHERE PABLO PICASSO'S CUBIST MASTERPIECE *THE PRODIGAL SON* ONCE HUNG...

IT WAS STOLEN IN 2012 BY THE INTERNATIONAL ART THIEF KNOWN AS REDMOND.
THE GALLERY HAS VOWED TO LEAVE THE FRAME HANGING EMPTY UNTIL THE PAINTING IS RECOVERED AND RETURNED TO ITS RIGHTFUL PLACE.
NOW IF YOU'LL FOLLOW ME THIS WAY...
BZZT BZZT
IS THIS LINE SECURE?
I DOUBT IT. WHAT DO YOU WANT, FOXLEY?
I TOLD YOU, YOU WEREN'T PAYING CELIA ENOUGH. SHE'S JUST BEEN ARRESTED.
AS REDMOND.
I THINK WE SHOULD--
BIP
FOXLEY

DEPARTMENT OF JUSTICE
FEDERAL BUREAU OF INVESTIGATION
WHITTAKER. FEDERAL PROSECUTOR.
I'M BEVERLEY SHANNON, SPECIAL AGENT IN--
I KNOW WHO YOU ARE. I'M HERE TO SEE YOU DON'T *FUCK IT UP* THIS TIME.
... *EXCUSE* ME?
YOU'RE *NATHAN DOUGLAS,* RIGHT? YOU WERE PARTNERED WITH *WHATSERNAME,* GOT HERSELF *FIRED.*
MADE US LOOK LIKE A BUNCH OF *ASSHOLES.*
UH...
I'M GONNA NEED EVERYTHING YOU'VE GOT ON REDMOND.
... WITH ALL DUE RESPECT, WE'RE STILL REVIEWING THE FACTS OF THE--
STOP.

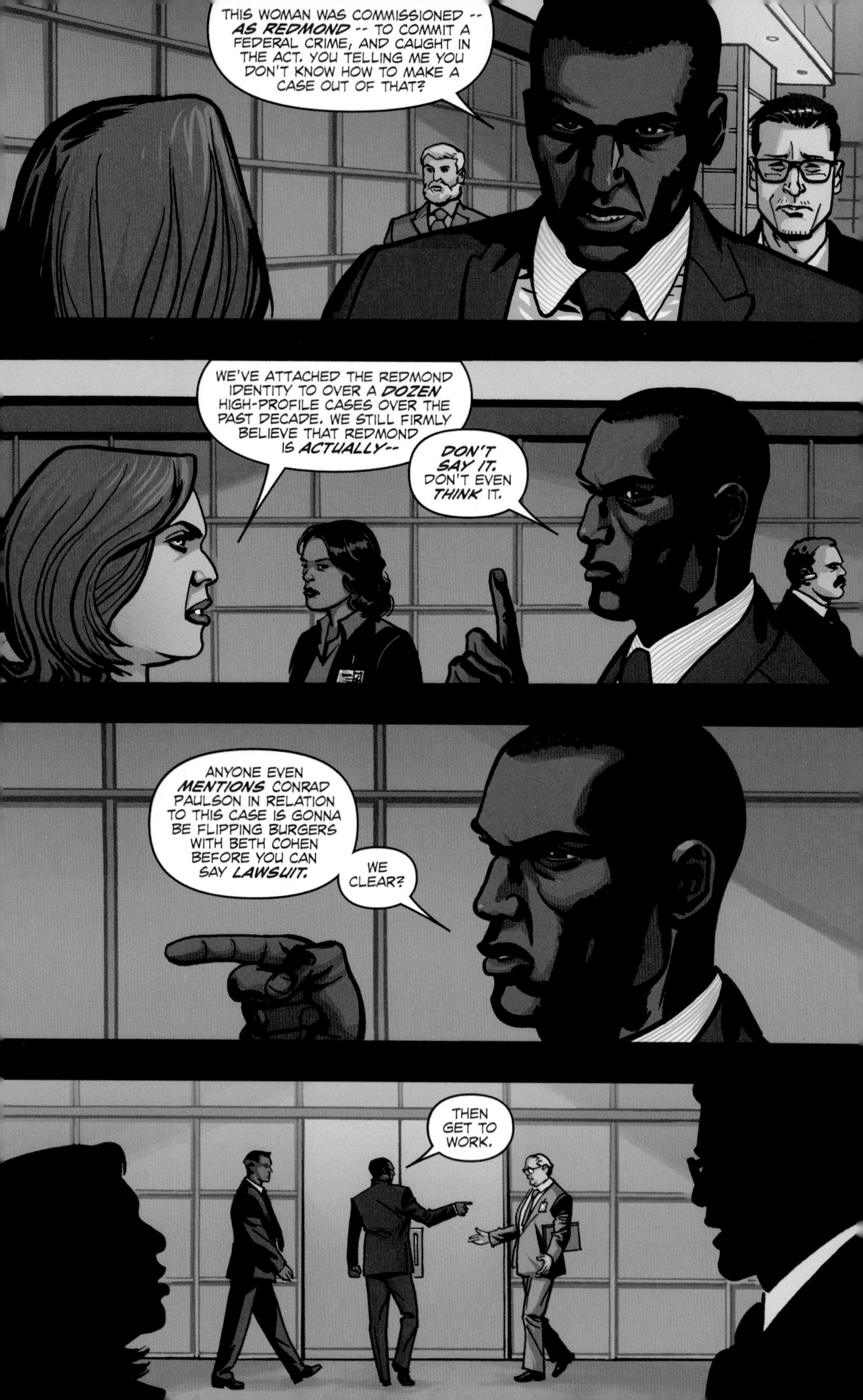
THIS WOMAN WAS COMMISSIONED -- AS REDMOND -- TO COMMIT A FEDERAL CRIME, AND CAUGHT IN THE ACT. YOU TELLING ME YOU DON'T KNOW HOW TO MAKE A CASE OUT OF THAT?
WE'VE ATTACHED THE REDMOND IDENTITY TO OVER A DOZEN HIGH-PROFILE CASES OVER THE PAST DECADE. WE STILL FIRMLY BELIEVE THAT REDMOND IS ACTUALLY--
DON'T SAY IT. DON'T EVEN THINK IT.
ANYONE EVEN MENTIONS CONRAD PAULSON IN RELATION TO THIS CASE IS GONNA BE FLIPPING BURGERS WITH BETH COHEN BEFORE YOU CAN SAY LAWSUIT.
WE CLEAR?
THEN GET TO WORK.

SO WE CLEAN?
YEP. NO PRYIN' EYES. NO WINDOWS TO BOUNCE A LASER MIC. NOBODY GETS IN OR OUT, WE DON'T KNOW ABOUT IT.
VERY WELL. THANK YOU ALL FOR COMING.
I APOLOGIZE FOR THE INCONVENIENCE, BUT GIVEN THE GRAVITY OF THE SITUATION, I CONSIDERED A PERSONAL TÊTE-À-TÊTE PREFERABLE TO ENTRUSTING OUR SECURITY TO THE VAGARIES OF POTENTIALLY COMPROMISED ONLINE COMMUNICATIONS--
WHAT IT IS, MAN'S SAYIN' WE GOTTA TALK ABOUT THE *CELIA PROBLEM.*

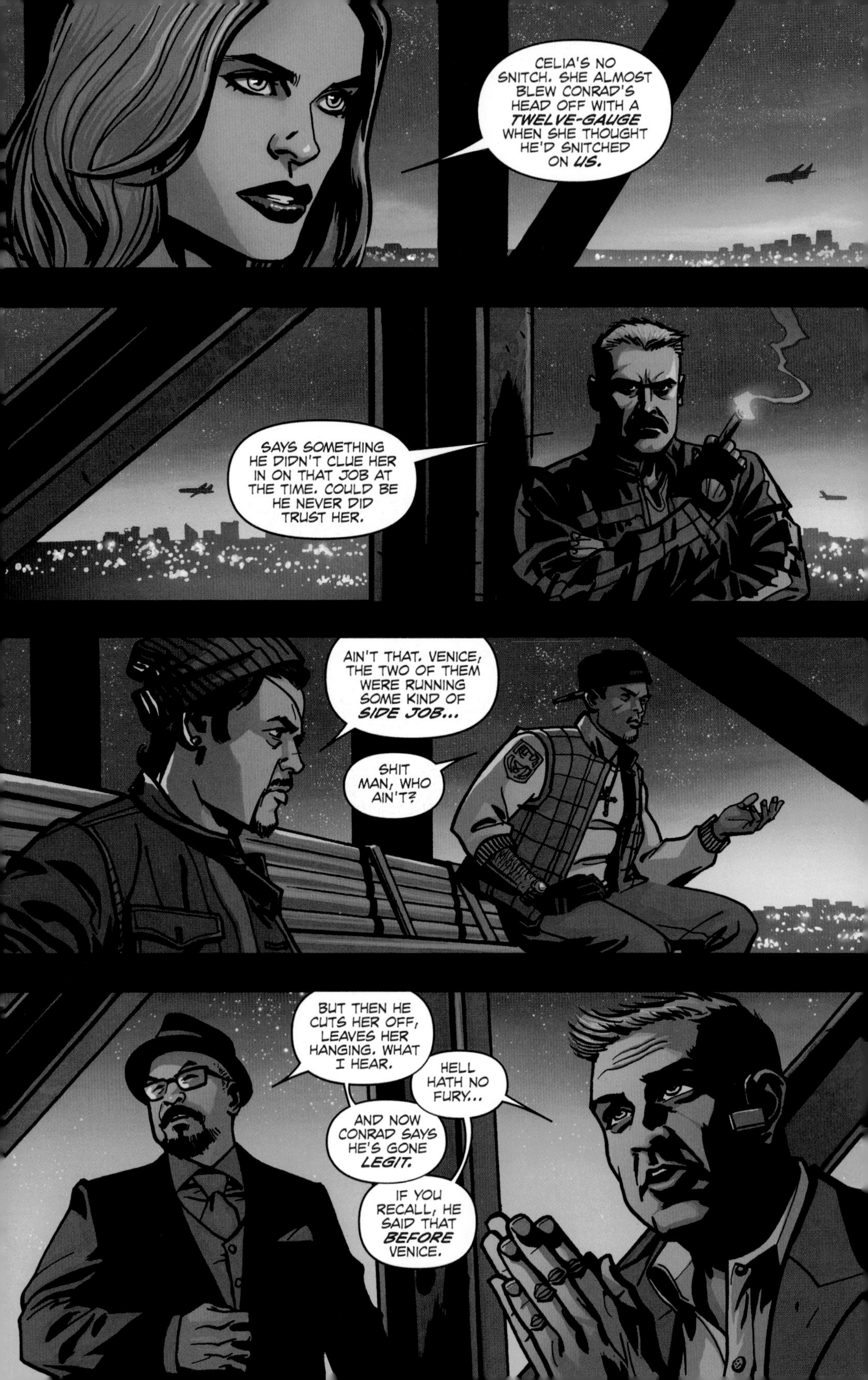
CELIA'S NO SNITCH. SHE ALMOST BLEW CONRAD'S HEAD OFF WITH A TWELVE-GAUGE WHEN SHE THOUGHT HE'D SNITCHED ON US.
SAYS SOMETHING HE DIDN'T CLUE HER IN ON THAT JOB AT THE TIME. COULD BE HE NEVER DID TRUST HER.
AIN'T THAT. VENICE, THE TWO OF THEM WERE RUNNING SOME KIND OF SIDE JOB...
SHIT MAN, WHO AIN'T?
BUT THEN HE CUTS HER OFF, LEAVES HER HANGING. WHAT I HEAR.
HELL HATH NO FURY...
AND NOW CONRAD SAYS HE'S GONE LEGIT.
IF YOU RECALL, HE SAID THAT BEFORE VENICE.

CAN'T TRUST AN HONEST MAN.
HONEST MY DICK. MOTHERFUCKER LEFT A TRAIL OF BODIES SIZE OF THE I-75.
FUCK IT. MAYBE WE SHOULD WHACK 'EM BOTH.
YOU'RE WELCOME TO TRY.
SHIT, GRANDIN. I THOUGHT YOU SAID THIS PLACE WAS SECURE!
FROM ME? PLEASE.

S'OKAY, GOT MY OWN SECURITY RIGHT HERE.
CHILL, BROTHER. I GOT INTO THIS GAME TO GET AWAY FROM THAT BODYBAG SHIT...
JUST TELL US THERE ISN'T A SWAT TEAM BACKING YOU UP RIGHT NOW, CONRAD.
YOU KNOW ME BETTER THAN THAT.
THOUGHT I DID.
LISTEN, YOU CAME THROUGH FOR US IN VENICE. HAD YOUR RESERVATIONS, BUT YOU STEPPED UP. I RESPECT THAT...
SO WHY DON'T YOU TRUST ME NOW?
TELL US WHAT HAPPENED TO ARNO, WE CAN TALK ABOUT TRUST.

LISTEN, YOU DON'T WANT TO INVITE ME TO YOUR LITTLE CLUBHOUSE? FINE, I GET IT.
BUT YOU NEED TO UNDERSTAND THAT I HAVE MORE TO LOSE THAN ANY OF YOU.
CELIA HAS A KID. SHE'S LOOKING AT HARD TIME. PRESSURE LIKE THAT, SOONER OR LATER...
WE WOULD BE LIVING BENEATH THE PROVERBIAL SWORD OF DAMOCLES.
BOTTOM LINE. SHE GOT SLOPPY. SHE GOT CAUGHT.
IT'S NOTHING PERSONAL.
IT IS TO ME.
SHE STOLE MY NAME. MY REPUTATION...

LEAVE CELIA TO ME.

HELLO, EMMA. HOW HAVE YOU BEEN?
HAVE YOU GOT PEOPLE ***FOLLOWING*** ME?
WHY DO YOU ASK?
I DUNNO, I JUST...
SOMETIMES IT FEELS LIKE I'M BEING ***WATCHED.***

SOUNDS TO ME LIKE A GUILTY CONSCIENCE. PERHAPS YOU SHOULD *UNBURDEN* YOURSELF.
IT'S LIKE I TOLD YOU, EMMA. IF YOU WANT ME TO EVEN *CONSIDER* YOU FOR WITNESS PROTECTION, FIRST YOU HAVE TO *EARN* IT.
FUCK'S *SAKE,* NATHAN! I'VE ALREADY *TOLD* YOU EVERYTHING I *KNOW--!*
THIS ISN'T ABOUT WHAT WENT DOWN IN SAN DIEGO. THIS IS SOMETHING ELSE.
WHEN DID YOU LAST SEE AUGUSTUS OR CONRAD PAULSON?
LIKE I *SAID,* WE'RE *HISTORY.* AUG BAILED *MONTHS* AGO. FLAT-OUT *DISAPPEARED* ON ME.
HE DOESN'T KNOW A GOOD THING WHEN HE'S GOT IT? FUCK HIM. I'VE MOVED ON. HIGHER GROUND.
DO YOU KNOW THIS WOMAN?

NEVER SEEN HER BEFORE.
THEN I GUESS WE'RE THROUGH. GOOD LUCK WITH THE CARTEL--
WAIT! JUST--
LEMME SEE IT AGAIN...
I NEVER MET HER, BUT AUG SAID SOMETHING ABOUT SOMEONE HIS DAD WORKED WITH. TATTOOS, PIERCINGS...
I GUESS THIS COULD BE HER...
HE SAID HER NAME'S CELIA.

STILL SMARTING FROM THAT BAIL HEARING? I DON'T THINK THE JUDGE WAS TOO IMPRESSED WITH YOUR REFUSAL TO IDENTIFY YOURSELF.
THAT'S OKAY. BAIL'S FOR PUSSIES. YOU'RE A TOUGH GIRL, YOU CAN HANDLE IT, CAN'T YOU...
... CELIA.
FUCK.

"CELIA JOZEFINA MAGDALINA KOWALCZYK."
QUITE A MOUTHFUL. I CAN SEE WHY YOU CHANGED IT TO REDMOND. GOOD, STRONG AMERICAN NAME. LAND OF OPPORTUNITY, AM I RIGHT?
SEEMS WE HAD YOU IN THE SYSTEM ALL ALONG. PETTY THEFT, RESISTING ARREST, POSSESSION. NOTHING HEAVY...
THEN A FEW YEARS AGO, ALL OF A SUDDEN -- BOOM. NOTHING. LIKE YOU JUST FELL OFF THE GRID.
SAN DIEGO
LET ME GUESS. THAT'S WHEN YOU DECIDED TO BECOME REDMOND.

ONE THING, I'M CURIOUS. HOW'D YOU KEEP YOUR FINGERPRINTS OUT OF THE SYSTEM? HACK THE DATABASE?
MAN, I HOPE SO. 'CAUSE THAT'S ANOTHER FEW YEARS RIGHT THERE...
STILL DON'T FEEL LIKE SHARING? THAT'S OKAY.
THE LESS YOU COOPERATE, THE BETTER IT MAKES ME LOOK WHEN I PUT YOU AWAY FOR THE REST OF YOUR NATURAL LIFE.
THIS IS BULLSHIT! NO WAY I'M LOOKING AT THAT KIND OF TIME.
I MEAN, CHRIST, IT'S NOT LIKE I KILLED ANYONE!
THAT WE KNOW OF. BUT I GOT PEOPLE LOOKING INTO IT, BELIEVE ME. YES I DO.
WE GOT A REDMOND FILE THE SIZE OF MY WIFE'S ASS. AND WE ARE GONNA DROP ALL OF IT...
... ON YOU.

UNLESS THERE'S SOMEONE ELSE I SHOULD BE TALKING TO?
... NO.
THAT'S GOOD. Y'KNOW WHY...?
I WANT IT TO BE YOU.

HA HA HA HA HA HA
MAN, THIS FEDERAL PROSECUTOR, THIS WHITTAKER -- IT'S LIKE HE'S SOME KIND OF NEXT-GENERATION ASSHOLE...
LIKE THE CHINESE ARE HACKING OUR SHIT TO LEARN HOW TO MAKE SOMEONE AS HYPER-EFFICIENT AT BEING A MASSIVE FUCKING DICK AS THIS GUY.
MY EXPERIENCE, TRUST ME, A MASSIVE DICK IS UNLIKELY TO BE HIS PROBLEM.
HE GETS SHIT DONE THOUGH, I'LL GIVE HIM THAT. EVERYONE WAS TOO SCARED TO MOVE UNTIL WHITTAKER MARCHES IN LIKE HE DOESN'T GIVE A GOOD GODDAMN...
AND SUDDENLY THE BALLOON'S GOING UP AND I'M LIKE, THE LONGER I HOLD ON, THE WORSE IT'S GONNA BE IF I LET GO.
... WHY WOULD YOU LET GO?

NATHAN. WHY DID YOU ASK ME HERE?
NO, I MEAN... IT'S NOT--
SHIT, HOW DO I PUT THIS...?
OKAY. ALRIGHT. ALL BULLSHIT ASIDE... LOOK, YOU'RE THE SMARTEST, MOST DRIVEN PERSON I EVER PARTNERED WITH. PERIOD.
WE WORKED REDMOND A LONG TIME TOGETHER. AND THEN... YOU DID WHAT YOU DID.
AND NOW THIS.
I GUESS I JUST NEED TO KNOW IF THERE'S ANYTHING I NEED TO KNOW.
Y'KNOW?
AND THERE WAS ME THINKING YOU JUST WANTED TO CATCH UP AND REMINISCE ABOUT OLD TIMES.

IT'S JUST... THIS PERSONAL OBSESSION OF YOURS WITH--
SO DID YOU!
PERSONAL? I WAS DOING MY JOB, NATHAN. CONRAD PAULSON BROKE THE LAW.
I GUESS THAT'S THE DIFFERENCE BETWEEN US. I WENT OUTSIDE THE LAW TO CATCH A MAN I KNEW TO BE GUILTY.
YOU'RE USING THE LAW TO PROSECUTE A WOMAN YOU KNOW TO BE INNOCENT.
INNOCENT?! SHE BROKE INTO THE--
SHE'S NOT REDMOND AND YOU KNOW IT.
ALL DUE RESPECT, LIZ, BUT FUCK WHAT I KNOW. WHAT I KNOW IS THAT YOU GOT YOURSELF FIRED AND THE BUREAU SUED FOR MILLIONS, AND FOR WHAT?
CHRIST, AFTER THAT SHIT YOU PULLED IN ITALY, IT'S A MIRACLE YOU'RE NOT IN JAIL!

I'M SORRY TO BE BLUNT, LIZ, BUT YOU'RE A *LIABILITY.*
THANKS.
SO TELL ME STRAIGHT. YOU OWE ME THIS MUCH AT LEAST...
WAS IT *YOU* WHO COMMISSIONED THIS LATEST REDMOND JOB?
I'M NOT THE ONE ON TRIAL, NATE. MAYBE TRY TO REMEMBER THAT.
YOU FIGURE OUT WHOSE SIDE YOU'RE ON, LET ME KNOW.

FINAL EXAM TODAY
SORRY.

IT'S OKAY. I THOUGHT I COULD JUST START OVER, BUT... I DUNNO.
I'M ACTUALLY GLAD YOU'RE HERE. THERE'S SOMETHING I'VE BEEN MEANING TO TELL YOU FOR A WHILE NOW...
YOU WERE *RIGHT.*
AUG--
NO, LISTEN. I NEED TO SAY THIS...
MY WHOLE LIFE, I *RESENTED* YOU. I WANTED TO BE JUST *LIKE* YOU, AND YOU KEPT ME AT ARM'S LENGTH.
AND IT FUCKING *HURT,* MAN. IT TWISTED ME UP INSIDE...
BUT ALL ALONG YOU WERE JUST TRYING TO *PROTECT* ME. I *GET* THAT NOW.

I GOT A TASTE OF YOUR WORLD, AND IT SCARED THE SHIT OUT OF ME. I THOUGHT IT'D BE FUN AND GAMES, BUT IT'S JUST BLOOD AND DEATH AND PAIN.
AUG, PLEASE--
SO I JUST WANTED TO SAY, THANK YOU. Y'KNOW? THANK YOU FOR STEERING ME AWAY FROM THAT SHIT.
I'D BE DEAD IF IT WASN'T FOR YOU.
SO I'M GOING STRAIGHT NOW, JUST LIKE YOU. WHETHER COLLEGE WORKS OUT, I DUNNO, BUT I FIGURE I'D MAKE A PRETTY GOOD SECURITY CONSULTANT.
I MEAN THAT'S YOUR THING, RIGHT? WE COULD WORK TOGETHER AND--
AUG.
I NEED YOU TO DO SOMETHING FOR ME.

WHAT... SORT OF THING?
OUR SORT OF THING.
... SO MUCH FOR RETIREMENT.
CHRIST, WHAT DID YOU LAST, A WEEK? YOU NEVER EVEN--
CELIA WAS ARRESTED.
... SHIT.

OKAY.

ONE HAIR BAND. SIX EARRINGS. ONE--
WHAT EVEN *IS* THIS?
IT'S AN *EYEBROW BAR.*
HUH.
I DON'T EVEN *WANT* TO KNOW WHERE THE *REST* OF THIS JUNK WENT.
WHAT ABOUT THE REST OF MY GEAR? BOOTS, WATCH, PHONE--?
EVIDENCE. YOU'LL GET IT BACK.
Y'KNOW.
EVENTUALLY.

WAKE UP'S AT FIVE. COUNT AT FIVE-THIRTY.
HAVE A NICE DAY.
KLUNNGG
HI, HONEY. I'M MARIE.
OH, ARE WE DOING THE STRONG, SILENT THING? SEE WHO GETS TO BE ALPHA BITCH...?
THAT'S ALRIGHT, HONEY, YOU GO RIGHT AHEAD. I'M TOO OLD FOR THAT SORTA NONSENSE.

CELIA.
THERE YOU GO. WELL, IT'S A PLEASURE TO MEET YOU, CELIA. IT'S NICE TO HAVE A LITTLE COMPANY AROUND THE PLACE.
YOU WANT THE TOP BUNK, YOU GO RIGHT AHEAD. I CAN'T GET UP THERE ANYWAY, WHAT WITH MY HIP AND ALL.
SO WHAT ARE YOU *IN* FOR?
AMBITION, I GUESS.
HA! AIN'T THAT THE TRUTH.
WELL, I'M SURE YOU'LL GET ALONG JUST FINE IN HERE. IT AIN'T LIKE IN THE MOVIES. MOST FOLKS HERE ARE ACTUALLY PRETTY DECENT.
MY ADVICE, DO WHAT I DO. JUST GO WITH THE FLOW. IT'LL DO YOU NO GOOD TRYING TO FIGHT IT...

IT WON'T LOOK LIKE SUICIDE IF YOU FIGHT IT.

GGGKKH!
GGG--
SSHHH. LET IT GO, HONEY. JUST LET IT GO...

UHHF!
WHOKK
... LIDDLE BIDTH! BROKE BY FUGGIG DOZE!
FUGGIG KILL YOU --

Y'KNOW WHAT, MARIE? I CHANGED MY MIND...
RRRAAAAAGH--!
WHUNCHH
YOU TAKE THE TOP BUNK.

CHRIST. ANOTHER DAY, ANOTHER FED...
NO, I DON'T WANT A LAWYER.
NO, I WON'T CUT A DEAL.
WE DONE?
WE'RE JUST GETTING STARTED.
CONRAD--?!

IT'S OKAY, I'VE SWEPT THE ROOM. WE CAN SPEAK FREELY.
FUNNY THING ABOUT FEDERAL PRISONS. THEY'RE A LOT EASIER TO GET INTO THAN OUT OF.
FBI
WHAT ARE YOU DOING HERE?
THE VENICE CREW ARE... CONCERNED YOU MIGHT FLIP ON THEM.
THEY THINK I'M HERE TO KILL YOU.
AND...
... ARE YOU?

JESUS, CELIA.
I'M SORRY, BUT... AFTER VENICE, AFTER LOLA... I DON'T KNOW WHAT TO THINK.
I DON'T EVEN KNOW WHO YOU *ARE* ANYMORE.
I'M *REDMOND.*
WELL, IT'S ABOUT GODDAMN *TIME.*

MY CELLMATE TRIED TO KILL ME LAST WEEK. DON'T SUPPOSE YOU KNOW ANYTHING ABOUT THAT?
I'LL LOOK INTO IT. HAVE THEY PUT YOU IN SOLITARY FOR PROTECTION?
NOPE. RECKON THE FEDS WOULDN'T SHED A TEAR IF I WOUND UP DEAD IN HERE.
TIE UP THE REDMOND FILES WITH A NEAT LITTLE BOW, Y'KNOW?
JUST KEEP YOUR HEAD DOWN AND TAKE CARE OF YOURSELF. DON'T DO ANYTHING THAT'LL BUY YOU EXTRA TIME.
SO YOU GOT A PLAN? TELL ME YOU GOT A PLAN.
PLEASE. IT'S *ME.*

THEY'RE FAST-TRACKING YOUR TRIAL. THEY BAGGED YOU ON THE FUSION JOB, BUT FRANKLY I DOUBT THEY'LL WANT TO TAKE THAT TO OPEN COURT...
FBI
SURE, BUT WHAT ABOUT THE REST OF IT? THEY'RE GONNA HIT ME WITH EVERY *REDMOND* JOB WE EVER PULLED TOGETHER!
LET THEM TRY.
NOW LISTEN UP. THERE'S A LOT TO TALK ABOUT AND WE DON'T HAVE MUCH TIME.
SPEAK FOR YOURSELF. SOMEPLACE YOU GOTTA BE?
YEAH...
VENICE.

< QUESTIONS ARE BEING ASKED ABOUT WHICH MASTER YOU TRULY SERVE, FERRARA. >
< AFTER THE *REDMOND* FIASCO, WE HAD TO MAKE IT *LOOK* LIKE WE WERE ACTING AGAINST PARRINO'S ORGANIZATION. >
< CERTAIN... *OFFICIAL NICETIES* HAD TO BE OBSERVED. >
< OBSERVED, AND NOTED. >
< I UNDERSTAND YOUR CONCERNS, DON SALVATORE. AFTER PARRINO'S DEATH, HIS MANSION WAS RAIDED, HIS POSSESSIONS IMPOUNDED. >
< I DON'T LIKE PAPER TRAILS, FERRARA... >
< REST EASY. HIS ART TREASURES DO NOT APPEAR ON *ANY* POLICE MANIFEST. >
< I SAW TO IT *PERSONALLY.* >

‹ ... AND NOW I BEQUEATH THEM TO YOU, DON SALVATORE. ›
‹ I TRUST YOU WILL TAKE THIS AS A TOKEN OF MY *LOYALTY* AND *RESPECT.* ›
‹ MOTHER OF GOD... ›
‹ YOU SAW TO IT PERSONALLY, *EH?* ›

< I THINK THAT IS EVERYTHING, YES? >
< SIGN HERE. >
< THANKS. >
4 127540 10 2
3 400-9 17 3
REDMOND

LIKE THE VIEW?
BETTER GET USED TO IT.
MAKE IT FAST, WHITTAKER. CAN'T YOU SEE I'M BUSY?
I GOT THINGS TO DO, PLACES TO GO...
KEEP TELLING YOURSELF THAT.
IT'S NOT ME NEEDS TELLING. IT'S SYSTEM DYNAMIC'S LEGAL DEPARTMENT.
... WHAT?

REACTOR PLANS? RING A BELL? SEE, TURNS OUT THERE'S ALL KINDS OF LAWS ABOUT THAT STUFF.
BUILDING A NUCLEAR FUSION DEVICE IN THE MIDDLE OF A MAJOR AMERICAN CITY WITHOUT ADEQUATE SECURITY PRECAUTIONS...
AND THAT'S BEFORE WE EVEN GET INTO THEIR MANY, MANY SAFETY VIOLATIONS AND BREACHES OF NON-PROLIFERATION PROTOCOL.
IF YOU THINK YOU CAN JUST--
AND LIKE YOU SAID, THEY WERE SUBSIDIZED BY THE FEDERAL GOVERNMENT.
YOU REALLY THINK THEY WANT ALL THAT AIRED IN OPEN COURT?
YOU THINK YOU'RE PRETTY SHARP.
TRY ME.

TELL ME. DOES YOUR SON THINK YOU'RE PRETTY SHARP...?
OR DOES HE KNOW YOU'RE JUST A COMMON CRIMINAL?
WHAT'S THE MATTER? NO SNAPPY COMEBACK?
GOOD. MY TURN.
Y'KNOW WHAT? FORGET THE REACTOR PLANS. I HAVE BIGGER FISH TO FRY...
HERE'S WHAT'S GOING TO HAPPEN. YOU'RE GOING TO PLEAD GUILTY TO THE REDMOND ART JOBS. ALL OF THEM.
YOU'RE GOING TO DO YOUR TIME...
... OR I'LL SEE TO IT THAT LITTLE LEROY SPENDS THE NEXT DECADE IN AN INSTITUTION.
A REALLY SHITTY ONE.

YOU SON OF A BITCH...
SHALL I TAKE THAT AS A YES?
... OKAY.
WHAT WAS THAT? I DIDN'T HEAR YOU.
I SAID OKAY! YOU GOT ME.
HAPPY NOW?
Y'KNOW WHAT...?
I'M GETTING THERE.

WHAT DO YOU MEAN, SYSTEM DYNAMIC ARE DROPPING CHARGES?!
RELAX, COHEN. YOU DODGED A BULLET.
I'M PLEASED TO REPORT THIS MEANS YOU WILL NO LONGER BE REQUIRED AS A MATERIAL WITNESS.
I HANDED YOU THAT CASE ON A GODDAMN PLATTER--!
EXCEPT CELIA WASN'T THE BIG FISH YOU WERE TRYING TO LAND, WAS SHE?
UNLESS YOU'RE STILL EXPECTING US TO BELIEVE YOU JUST STUMBLED ACROSS THIS "REDMOND" ON THE DARKNET AND, WHAT, BROUGHT IT TO DYNAMIC'S ATTENTION OUT OF THE GOODNESS OF YOUR HEART?
ALL DUE RESPECT, BUT GO F--
UH, MS. COHEN HAS NO FURTHER COMMENT TO MAKE AT THIS TIME.

THIS IS GOOD FOR US. IT'S CLEAN.
ALL THE TIME, MONEY, MANPOWER YOU PEOPLE WASTED CHASING CONRAD PAULSON -- ALL THE FACE YOU LOST -- WE WIN IT ALL BACK HERE.
EVERY JOB YOU SAID HE EVER DID, WE LAY IT ON CELIA.
AND SHE'LL LIE DOWN AND TAKE IT. YES SHE WILL.
AND IF HER CREW HAVE HER KILLED BEFORE SHE MAKES IT BACK TO PRISON?
THEN WE WON'T NEED TO WORRY ABOUT A RETRIAL, WILL WE?

WOULD THE DEFENDANT PLEASE IDENTIFY HERSELF FOR THE COURT.
SAN DIEGO
CELIA JOSEFINA MAGDALENA KOWALCZYC.
I UNDERSTAND YOU HAVE WAIVED YOUR RIGHT TO COUNSEL. IS THAT CORRECT?
YES, MA'AM.
VERY WELL...
YOU STAND ACCUSED OF TWENTY-SEVEN COUNTS OF GRAND LARCENY WHILE OPERATING UNDER THE ALIAS OF *"REDMOND."*
HOW DO YOU PLEAD?

NOT GUILTY.
SON OF A BITCH.
TOLDJA.
AND I UNDERSTAND YOU WILL BE INTRODUCING NO WITNESSES ON BEHALF OF YOUR DEFENSE...?
JUST ONE, YOUR HONOR. A LATE ADDITION...

THE DEFENSE CALLS CONRAD PAULSON.

CONRAD PAULSON, DO YOU SOLEMNLY SWEAR THAT YOU WILL TELL THE TRUTH, THE WHOLE TRUTH, AND NOTHING BUT THE TRUTH, SO HELP YOU GOD?
YES I DO.
PLEASE BE SEATED.
WOULD YOU PLEASE TELL THE COURT WHAT LINE OF WORK YOU'RE IN, MR. PAULSON?
I'M A SECURITY CONSULTANT.
COOL. AND WHAT IS YOUR RELATIONSHIP TO THE DEFENDANT? THAT IS, *UH...*
... ME.
I'M YOUR LOVER.
... YES. YES, YOU ARE.
AWESOME. THANK YOU.

MS. KOWALCZYC, THIS IS SOMEWHAT IRREGULAR...
I UNDERSTAND YOU ARE STANDING AS YOUR OWN COUNSEL, BUT YOU'RE SUPPOSED TO MAKE A DEFENSE STATEMENT *PRIOR* TO DEPOSING WITNESSES.
I UNDERSTAND, YOUR HONOR. BUT TRUST ME, THIS IS AS MUCH ABOUT CONRAD HERE AS IT IS ABOUT ME.
THE F.B.I. ARE ACCUSING ME OF BEING A LEGENDARY *THIEF* THEY CALL ***REDMOND.***
BUT I'M NOT THE FIRST PERSON THEY'VE ACCUSED...
DON'T YOU GO THERE.

I MYSELF WAS TWICE ACCUSED OF BEING REDMOND. IN BOTH INSTANCES, I SUCCESSFULLY SUED THE F.B.I. FOR WRONGFUL ARREST.
THE SETTLEMENTS WERE... SUBSTANTIAL.
AND WHO WAS RESPONSIBLE FOR THESE MISCARRIAGES OF JUSTICE?
SHE'S SITTING RIGHT THERE.
SHE'S A FEDERAL AGENT. OR WAS, BEFORE SHE WAS FIRED.
HER NAME IS ELIZABETH COHEN.

"COHEN BECAME INFATUATED WITH ME. OBSESSED. SHE BEGAN STALKING ME. ON ONE OCCASION, SHE ACTUALLY SNUCK INTO MY HOUSE.
"I WOKE TO FIND HER IN MY KITCHEN, UNINVITED, COOKING HERSELF BREAKFAST...
"SHE LATER FOLLOWED ME ON VACATION, FALSELY CLAIMING TO BE IN ITALY ON OFFICIAL F.B.I. BUSINESS.
"IT'S SINCE COME TO LIGHT THAT SHE WAS COLLUDING WITH AN ITALIAN POLICE OFFICER WHO TURNED OUT TO BE IN THE EMPLOY OF THE MAFIA.
"SHE KILLED HIM.
"UNDERSTANDABLY, SHE WAS DISMISSED FOR GROSS MISCONDUCT. THOUGH HOW SHE DIDN'T END UP IN JAIL, I'LL NEVER KNOW."

YOUR HONOR, I BELIEVE THE DEFENDANT IS TRYING TO PROVOKE MS. COHEN INTO MAKING AN UNGUARDED STATEMENT.
IF SHE WISHES TO CALL HER AS A WITNESS, THAT IS HER RIGHT. BUT I WOULD REMIND THE COURT THAT MS. COHEN IS NOT PRESENTLY UNDER OATH.
I'M QUITE AWARE OF THAT, MR. WHITTAKER.
MS. KOWALCZYC, WOULD YOU MIND TELLING US WHAT RELEVANCE ANY OF THIS HAS TO DO WITH THE CHARGES AGAINST YOURSELF?
ISN'T IT OBVIOUS? ELIZABETH COHEN HAS AN OBSESSIVE, PSYCHOSEXUAL FIXATION WITH MY BOYFRIEND.
WHEN HE REJECTED HER, SHE MADE UP THIS REDMOND STORY TO TRY AND DESTROY HIS LIFE!
INSTEAD, SHE ENDED UP DESTROYING HER OWN. SHE WAS DISCREDITED. DISGRACED. A LAUGHING STOCK...
AND THAT'S WHEN SHE GOT HER FEDERAL FRIENDS TO DIRECT HER REDMOND ACCUSATIONS AT ME -- THE WOMAN WHO HAD TAKEN FROM HER THE ONLY THING SHE HAD EVER TRULY WANTED...

CONRAD PAULSON.
SLAM!
THINK I HIT A NERVE.
WE WILL ADJOURN FOR ONE HOUR BEFORE WE HEAR THE PROSECUTION'S STATEMENT.

MS. KOWALCZYC WANTS TO MISLEAD YOU WITH COUNTER-ACCUSATIONS THAT HAVE NOTHING WHATSOEVER TO DO WITH THE CHARGES AGAINST HER.
BUT ONCE WE PENETRATE THAT SMOKESCREEN, YOU WILL SEE THAT CELIA KOWALCZYC IS A HIGHLY-TRAINED PROFESSIONAL THIEF WITH AN INTERNATIONAL REPUTATION.
THAT REPUTATION WAS BUILT ON THE THEFT OF OVER A DOZEN MAJOR WORKS OF ART...
... REACHING ITS ZENITH WITH THE THEFT FROM THE SAN DIEGO GALLERY OF PABLO PICASSO'S CUBIST MASTERPIECE, THE PRODIGAL SON.
THE PAINTING SOLD AT AUCTION FOR TWELVE MILLION DOLLARS--
THE SPACE IN THE GALLERY WHERE IT HUNG HAS BEEN LEFT EMPTY FOR YEARS AS A--
KKRRZZZTT
AS A MARK OF RESPECT FOR--
KZZTTT
WHAT THE HELL IS THIS...?
HAVEN'T YOU GUESSED, MR. WHITTAKER?
IT'S REDMOND.

... HUH.
SEAL OFF THE BUILDING! THREE BLOCK CORDON! AND GET TECH SERVICES DOWN HERE!
THERE'S A SIGNAL GOING OUT OF THIS ROOM, AND I WANT IT TRACED!
I THINK WE SHOULD CLEAR THE ROOM.
CLERK OF THE COURT...?
I REALLY WOULDN'T DO THAT IF I WERE YOU, YOUR HONOR. THE COURTROOM IS WIRED...
... AND I'D HATE FOR YOU TO MISS THE SHOW.

WHAT DO YOU WANT?
I WANT YOU TO STOP ACCUSING RANK AMATEURS OF BEING ME.
IT'S EMBARRASSING. I HAVE A REPUTATION TO MAINTAIN.
AND WE'RE SUPPOSED TO JUST... TRUST THAT YOU'RE REDMOND, IS THAT RIGHT?
A MAN IN A MASK.
THIS IS A COURT OF LAW YOU'VE HACKED INTO. WE DEAL IN PROOF.
SO WHAT YOU'RE SAYING IS, YOU'D LIKE A DEMONSTRATION...?
WAAAY AHEAD OF YOU.
THAT'S THE GALLERY. THE SAN DIEGO GALLERY--!
SEND UNITS! SEND EVERYTHING! GO!
WELL, THIS IS ALL VERY EXCITING.

MMPH--!

BING BONG!
LEROY.
HE-- I--
TH-THERE'S NO ONE HERE BY THAT NAME.
SEARCH IT.

M-MOMMY...?
ARE YOU... GOING TO ARREST ME?
... I HAVEN'T DECIDED YET.

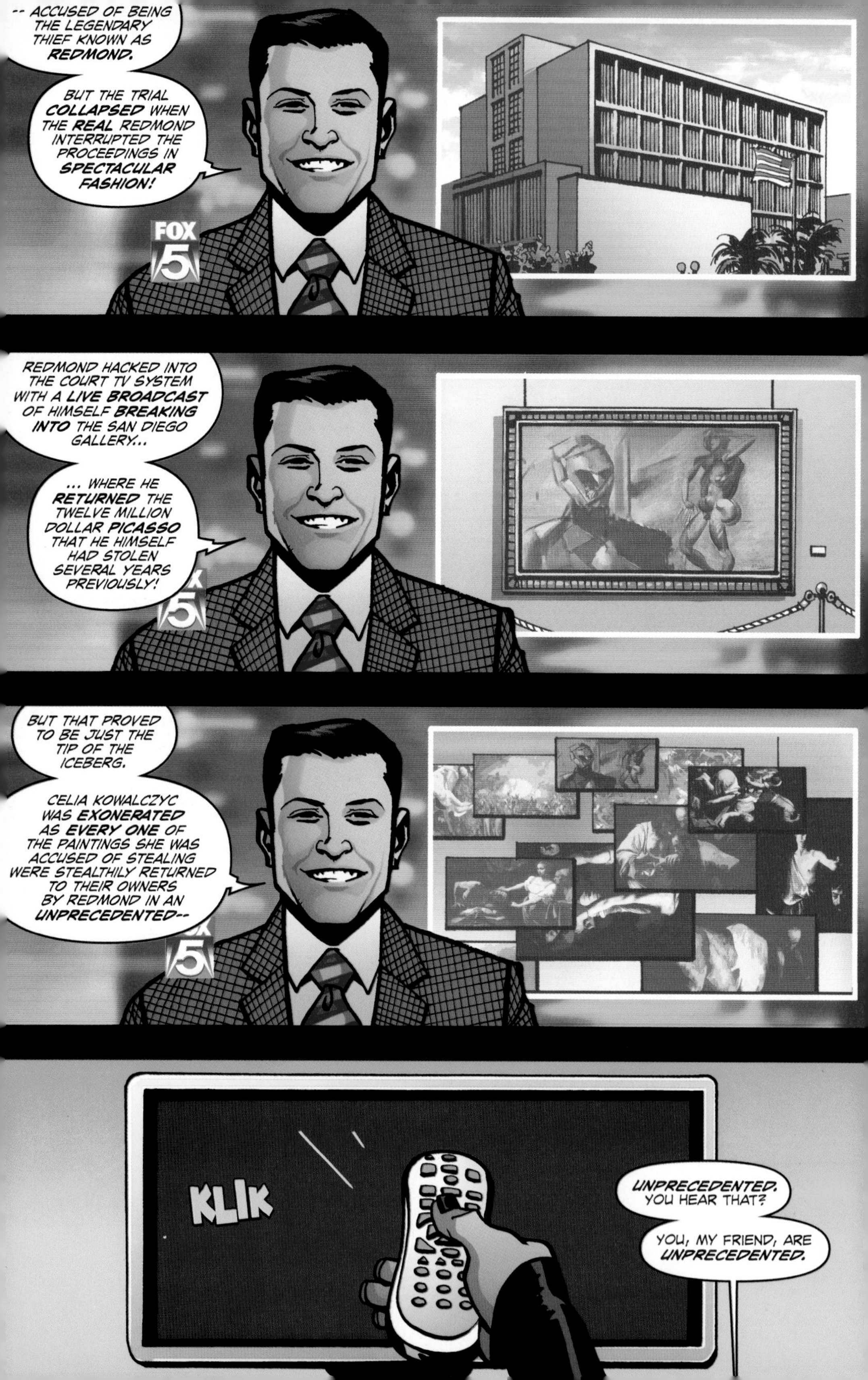
-- ACCUSED OF BEING THE LEGENDARY THIEF KNOWN AS REDMOND.
BUT THE TRIAL COLLAPSED WHEN THE REAL REDMOND INTERRUPTED THE PROCEEDINGS IN SPECTACULAR FASHION!
FOX 5
REDMOND HACKED INTO THE COURT TV SYSTEM WITH A LIVE BROADCAST OF HIMSELF BREAKING INTO THE SAN DIEGO GALLERY...
... WHERE HE RETURNED THE TWELVE MILLION DOLLAR PICASSO THAT HE HIMSELF HAD STOLEN SEVERAL YEARS PREVIOUSLY!
BUT THAT PROVED TO BE JUST THE TIP OF THE ICEBERG.
CELIA KOWALCZYC WAS EXONERATED AS EVERY ONE OF THE PAINTINGS SHE WAS ACCUSED OF STEALING WERE STEALTHILY RETURNED TO THEIR OWNERS BY REDMOND IN AN UNPRECEDENTED--
KLIK
UNPRECEDENTED. YOU HEAR THAT?
YOU, MY FRIEND, ARE UNPRECEDENTED.

ME? I SAT THERE IN COURT THE WHOLE TIME.
NO, THE CREDIT HAS TO GO TO REDMOND HIMSELF...
TO AUGUSTUS!
JEEZ, DAD. GIMME A BREAK. I WAS, Y'KNOW...
... JUST FOLLOWING ORDERS.
NO NEED TO BE MODEST, SON. THERE'S FEW MEN IN THE WORLD WHO COULD PULL OFF WHAT YOU DID.

I'M GLAD YOU'RE HAPPY.
I'M GLAD I'M NOT IN *JAIL.*
LOOK, YOU GUYS ENJOY THE SPOILS OF VICTORY OR WHATEVER. I'M GONNA HEAD ON UP.
YOU'RE NOT GONNA CELEBRATE WITH YOUR OLD MAN? I THOUGHT THIS WAS WHAT YOU ALWAYS WANTED, ISN'T IT?
...
SURE, DAD. I'M JUST TIRED.
G'NIGHT.
KID'S A LIGHTWEIGHT.
AND YOU'RE A FUNCTIONAL ALCOHOLIC. CUT HIM SOME SLACK.
I'M A *WHAT...?*
RELAX, YOU'RE IN GOOD COMPANY FOR IT.
BUT I BET YOU DIDN'T TOUCH A DROP WHILE YOU WERE STEALING BACK THOSE PAINTINGS FOR AUG TO RETURN, DID YOU?
... NO.

THERE'S ONLY EVER BEEN ONE THING THAT CAN FILL THE HOLE FOR YOU. WE BOTH KNOW IT...
IF YOU'RE TRYING TO CONVINCE ME TO TAKE UP THE LIFE OF CRIME AGAIN, YOU CAN SAVE YOUR BREATH.
WHY, 'CAUSE YOU QUIT ALREADY? I BELIEVE I HEARD THAT ONE BEFORE...
NO. BECAUSE I'VE ALREADY MADE UP MY MIND.
YOU WERE RIGHT, WHAT YOU SAID BEFORE. IT USED TO BE FUN. IT IS FUN.
QUITTING IS FOR QUITTERS...
HERE'S TO CRIME.

OH! HEY, LEROY. WHAT'S UP? CAN'T SLEEP...?
MOMMY'S BEING ALL LOUD. I DON'T LIKE IT WHEN SHE'S LOUD LIKE THAT.
SHE'S JUST EXCITED TO HAVE YOU BACK.
C'MON. LET'S GET YOU BACK TO BED. AND THEN TOMORROW YOU CAN HAVE MOMMY ALL TO YOURSELF.
FOR LIKE A *DAY.* AND THEN SHE'S GONNA GO *AWAY* AGAIN, JUST LIKE *ALWAYS.*

...
WELL, YOUR MOMMY HAS TO WORK. BUT YOU KNOW SHE *LOVES* YOU MORE THAN *ANYTHING,* RIGHT?
I GUESS. SHE SENDS ME TOYS SOMETIMES. THEY'RE REALLY BIG. BUT...
BUT YOU'D RATHER SHE WAS JUST HERE.
... YEAH.
I KNOW HOW YOU FEEL, BIG GUY. IT PRETTY MUCH SUCKS. BUT I WANT YOU TO KNOW...

I'VE GOT YOUR BACK.

TO BE CONTINUED...

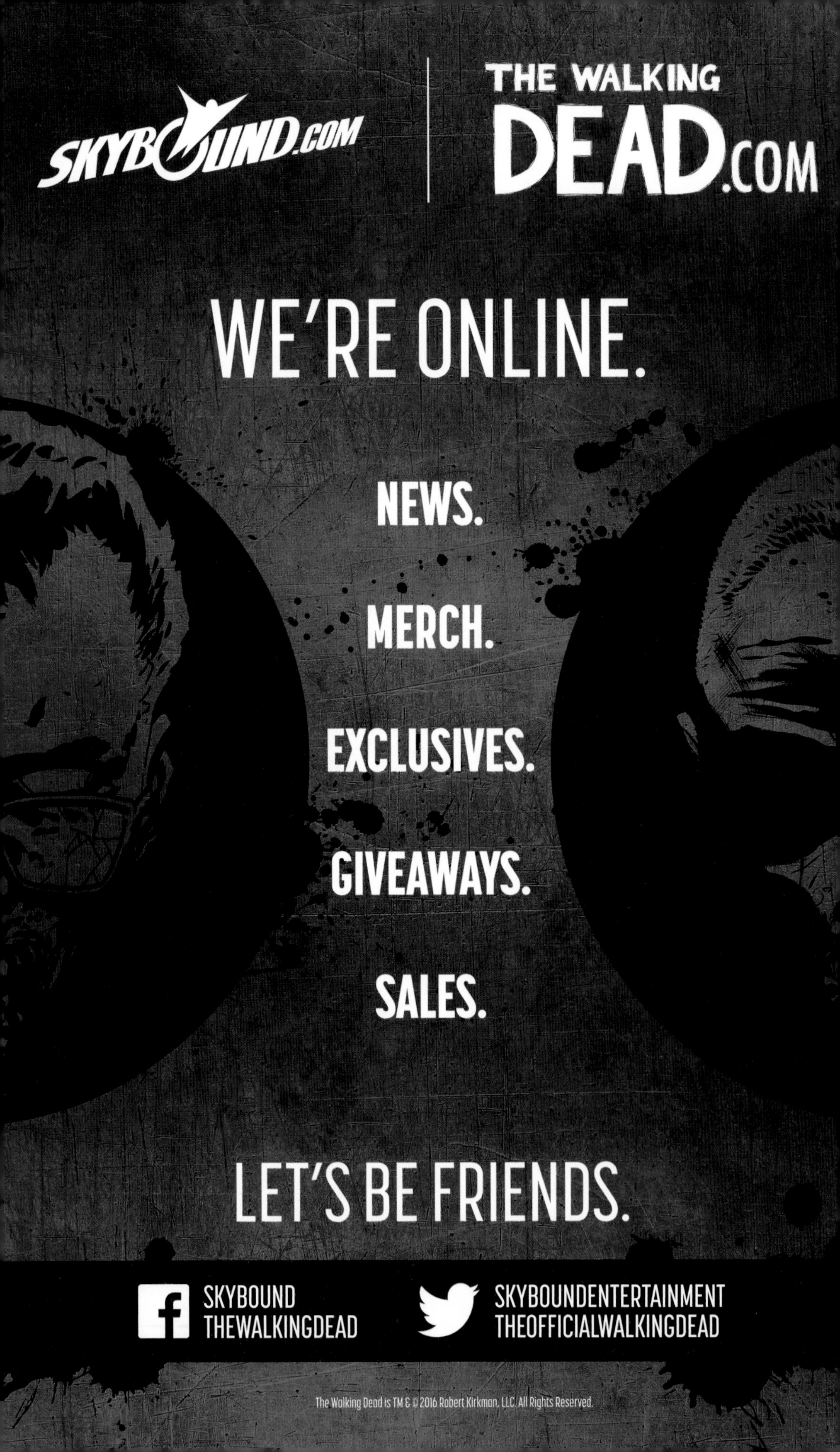
SKYBOUND.COM
THE WALKING DEAD.COM
WE'RE ONLINE.
NEWS.
MERCH.
EXCLUSIVES.
GIVEAWAYS.
SALES.
LET'S BE FRIENDS.
SKYBOUND
THEWALKINGDEAD
SKYBOUNDENTERTAINMENT
THEOFFICIALWALKINGDEAD
The Walking Dead is TM & © 2016 Robert Kirkman, LLC. All Rights Reserved.

SKYBOUND INSIDER

Join the **Skybound Insider** program and get updates on all of Skybound's great content including **The Walking Dead**.

- Get a **monthly** newsletter
- **Invites** to members-only events
- **Sneak peeks** of new comics
- **Discounts** on merchandise at the Skybound and Walking Dead online stores.

Membership is **free** and it only takes a minute to sign up.

BECOME A SKYBOUND INSIDER TODAY!

insider.skybound.com

All images and characters are ™ & © Skybound, LLC and/or Robert Kirkman, LLC 2016. All Rights Reserved.

FOR MORE OF THE WALKING DEAD

TRADEPAPERBACKS

VOL. 1: DAYS GONE BYE TP
ISBN: 978-1-58240-672-5
$14.99
VOL. 2: MILES BEHIND US TP
ISBN: 978-1-58240-775-3
$14.99
VOL. 3: SAFETY BEHIND BARS TP
ISBN: 978-1-58240-805-7
$14.99
VOL. 4: THE HEART'S DESIRE TP
ISBN: 978-1-58240-530-8
$14.99
VOL. 5: THE BEST DEFENSE TP
ISBN: 978-1-58240-612-1
$14.99
VOL. 6: THIS SORROWFUL LIFE TP
ISBN: 978-1-58240-684-8
$14.99
VOL. 7: THE CALM BEFORE TP
ISBN: 978-1-58240-828-6
$14.99
VOL. 8: MADE TO SUFFER TP
ISBN: 978-1-58240-883-5
$14.99
VOL. 9: HERE WE REMAIN TP
ISBN: 978-1-60706-022-2
$14.99
VOL. 10: WHAT WE BECOME TP
ISBN: 978-1-60706-075-8
$14.99
VOL. 11: FEAR THE HUNTERS TP
ISBN: 978-1-60706-181-6
$14.99
VOL. 12: LIFE AMONG THEM TP
ISBN: 978-1-60706-254-7
$14.99
VOL. 13: TOO FAR GONE TP
ISBN: 978-1-60706-329-2
$14.99
VOL. 14: NO WAY OUT TP
ISBN: 978-1-60706-392-6
$14.99
VOL. 15: WE FIND OURSELVES TP
ISBN: 978-1-60706-440-4
$14.99
VOL. 16: A LARGER WORLD TP
ISBN: 978-1-60706-559-3
$14.99
VOL. 17: SOMETHING TO FEAR TP
ISBN: 978-1-60706-615-6
$14.99
VOL. 18: WHAT COMES AFTER TP
ISBN: 978-1-60706-687-3
$14.99
VOL. 19: MARCH TO WAR TP
ISBN: 978-1-60706-818-1
$14.99
VOL. 20: ALL OUT WAR PART ONE TP
ISBN: 978-1-60706-882-2
$14.99
VOL. 21: ALL OUT WAR PART TWO TP
ISBN: 978-1-63215-030-1
$14.99
VOL. 22: A NEW BEGINNING TP
ISBN: 978-1-63215-041-7
$14.99
VOL. 23: WHISPERS INTO SCREAMS TP
ISBN: 978-1-63215-258-9
$14.99
VOL. 24: LIFE AND DEATH TP
ISBN: 978-1-63215-402-6
$14.99
VOL. 25: NO TURNING BACK TP
ISBN: 978-1-63215-612-9
$14.99
VOL. 1: SPANISH EDITION TP
ISBN: 978-1-60706-797-
$14.99
VOL. 2: SPANISH EDITION TP
ISBN: 978-1-60706-845-
$14.99
VOL. 3: SPANISH EDITION TP
ISBN: 978-1-60706-883-
$14.99
VOL. 4: SPANISH EDITION TP
ISBN: 978-1-63215-035-
$14.99

HARDCOVERS

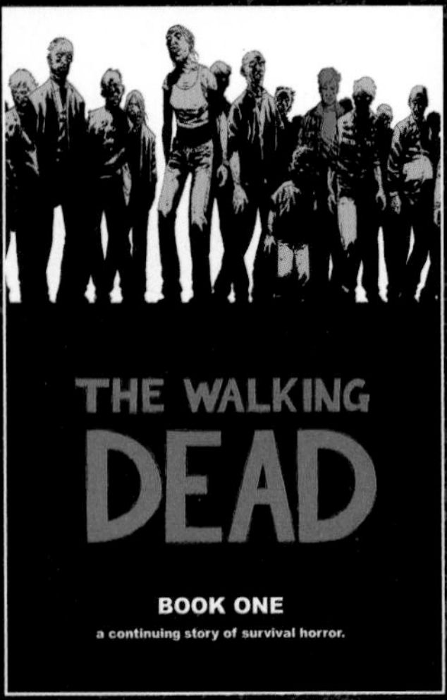

BOOK ONE HC
ISBN: 978-1-58240-619-0
$34.99
BOOK TWO HC
ISBN: 978-1-58240-698-5
$34.99
BOOK THREE HC
ISBN: 978-1-58240-825-5
$34.99
BOOK FOUR HC
ISBN: 978-1-60706-000-0
$34.99
BOOK FIVE HC
ISBN: 978-1-60706-171-7
$34.99
BOOK SIX HC
ISBN: 978-1-60706-327-8
$34.99
BOOK SEVEN HC
ISBN: 978-1-60706-439-8
$34.99
BOOK EIGHT HC
ISBN: 978-1-60706-593-7
$34.99
BOOK NINE HC
ISBN: 978-1-60706-798-6
$34.99
BOOK TEN HC
ISBN: 978-1-63215-034-9
$34.99
BOOK ELEVEN HC
ISBN: 978-1-63215-271-8
$34.99

COMPENDIUMS

COMPENDIUM TP, VOL. 1
ISBN: 978-1-60706-076-5
$59.99
COMPENDIUM TP, VOL. 2
ISBN: 978-1-60706-596-8
$59.99
COMPENDIUM TP, VOL. 3
ISBN: 978-1-63215-456-9
$59.99

SPECIALTY BOOKS

THE WALKING DEAD: THE COVERS, VOL. 1 HC
ISBN: 978-1-60706-002-4
$24.99
THE WALKING DEAD SURVIVORS' GUIDE
ISBN: 978-1-60706-458-9
$12.99
THE WALKING DEAD: ALL OUT WAR HC
ISBN: 978-1-63215-038-7
$34.99

OMNIBUS

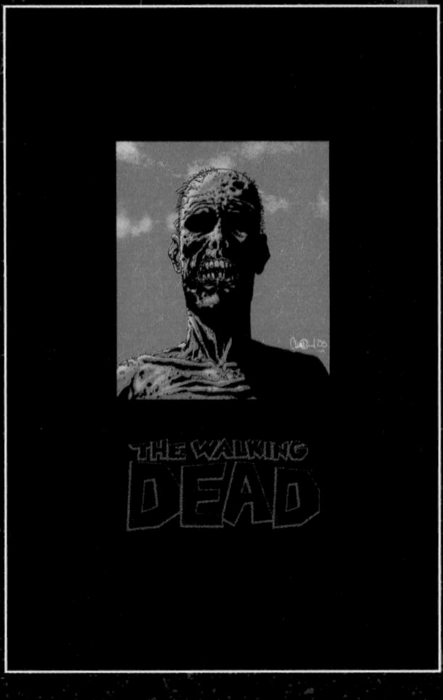

OMNIBUS, VOL. 1
ISBN: 978-1-60706-503-6
$100.00
OMNIBUS, VOL. 2
ISBN: 978-1-60706-515-9
$100.00
OMNIBUS, VOL. 3
ISBN: 978-1-60706-330-8
$100.00
OMNIBUS, VOL. 4
ISBN: 978-1-60706-616-3
$100.00
OMNIBUS, VOL. 5
ISBN: 978-1-63215-042-4
$100.00

FOR MORE OF INVINCIBLE

TRADEPAPERBACKS

VOL. 1: FAMILY MATTERS TP
ISBN: 978-1-58240-711-1
$12.99
VOL. 2: EIGHT IS ENOUGH TP
ISBN: 978-1-58240-347-2
$12.99
VOL. 3: PERFECT STRANGERS TP
ISBN: 978-1-58240-793-7
$12.99
VOL. 4: HEAD OF THE CLASS TP
ISBN: 978-1-58240-778-4
$14.99
VOL. 5: THE FACTS OF LIFE TP
ISBN: 978-1-58240-554-4
$14.99
VOL. 6: A DIFFERENT WORLD TP
ISBN: 978-1-58240-579-7
$14.99
VOL. 7: THREE'S COMPANY TP
ISBN: 978-1-58240-656-5
$14.99
VOL. 8: MY FAVORITE MARTIAN TP
ISBN: 978-1-58240-683-1
$16.99
VOL. 9: OUT OF THIS WORLD TP
ISBN: 978-1-58240-827-9
$14.99
VOL. 10: WHO'S THE BOSS TP
ISBN: 978-1-60706-013-0
$16.99
VOL. 11: HAPPY DAYS TP
ISBN: 978-1-60706-062-8
$16.99
VOL. 12: STILL STANDING TP
ISBN: 978-1-60706-166-3
$16.99
VOL. 13: GROWING PAINS TP
ISBN: 978-1-60706-251-6
$16.99
VOL. 14: THE VILTRUMITE WAR TP
ISBN: 978-1-60706-367-4
$19.99
VOL. 15: GET SMART TP
ISBN: 978-1-60706-498-5
$16.99
VOL. 16: FAMILY TIES TP
ISBN: 978-1-60706-579-1
$16.99
VOL. 17: WHAT'S HAPPENING TP
ISBN: 978-1-60706-662-0
$16.99
VOL. 18: DEATH OF EVERYONE TP
ISBN: 978-1-60706-762-7
$16.99
VOL. 19: THE WAR AT HOME TP
ISBN: 978-1-60706-856-3
$16.99
VOL. 20: FRIENDS TP
ISBN: 978-1-63215-043-1
$16.99
VOL. 21: MODERN FAMILY TP
ISBN: 978-1-63215-318-0
$16.99
VOL. 22: REBOOT? TP
ISBN: 978-1-63215-626-6
$16.99

THE OFFICIAL HANDBOOK OF
THE INVINCIBLE UNIVERSE TP
ISBN: 978-1-58240-831-6
$12.99
INVINCIBLE PRESENTS,
VOL. 1: ATOM EVE & REX SPLODE TP
ISBN: 978-1-60706-255-4
$14.99

COMPLETE LIBRARY

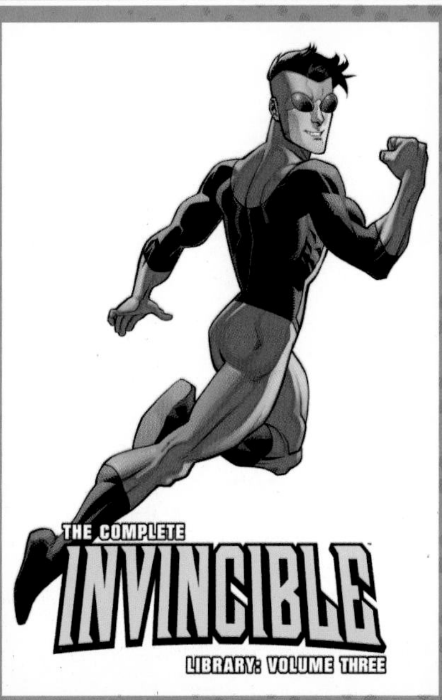

THE COMPLETE INVINCIBLE LIBRARY, VOL. 2 HC
ISBN: 978-1-60706-112-0
$125.00
THE COMPLETE INVINCIBLE LIBRARY, VOL. 3 HC
ISBN: 978-1-60706-421-3
$125.00

COMPENDIUMS

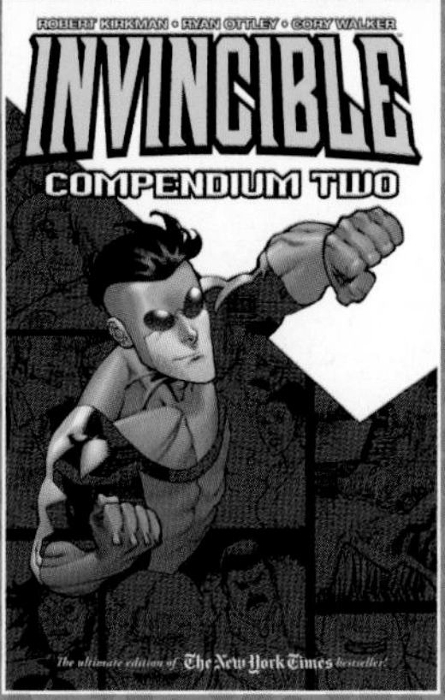

COMPENDIUM VOL. 1
ISBN: 978-1-60706-411-4
$64.99
COMPENDIUM VOL. 2
ISBN: 978-1-60706-772-6
$64.99

ULTIMATE COLLECTIONS

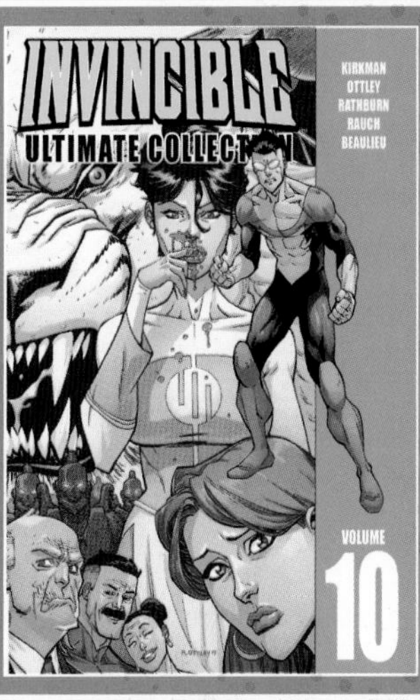

ULTIMATE COLLECTION, VOL. 1 HC
ISBN 978-1-58240-500-1
$34.99
ULTIMATE COLLECTION, VOL. 2 HC
ISBN: 978-1-58240-594-0
$34.99
ULTIMATE COLLECTION, VOL. 3 HC
ISBN: 978-1-58240-763-0
$34.99
ULTIMATE COLLECTION, VOL. 4 HC
ISBN: 978-1-58240-989-4
$34.99
ULTIMATE COLLECTION, VOL. 5 HC
ISBN: 978-1-60706-116-8
$34.99
ULTIMATE COLLECTION, VOL. 6 HC
ISBN: 978-1-60706-360-5
$34.99
ULTIMATE COLLECTION, VOL. 7 HC
ISBN: 978-1-60706-509-8
$39.99
ULTIMATE COLLECTION, VOL. 8 HC
ISBN: 978-1-60706-680-4
$39.99
ULTIMATE COLLECTION, VOL. 9 HC
ISBN: 978-1-63215-032-5
$39.99
ULTIMATE COLLECTION, VOL. 10 HC
ISBN: 978-1-63215-494-1
$39.99

INVINCIBLE™ © 2016 Robert Kirkman, LLC & Cory Walker.

FOR MORE TALES FROM ROBERT KIRKMAN AND SKYBOUND

VOL. 1: A DARKNESS SURROUNDS HIM TP
ISBN: 978-1-63215-053-0
$9.99

VOL. 2: A VAST AND UNENDING RUIN TP
ISBN: 978-1-63215-448-4
$14.99

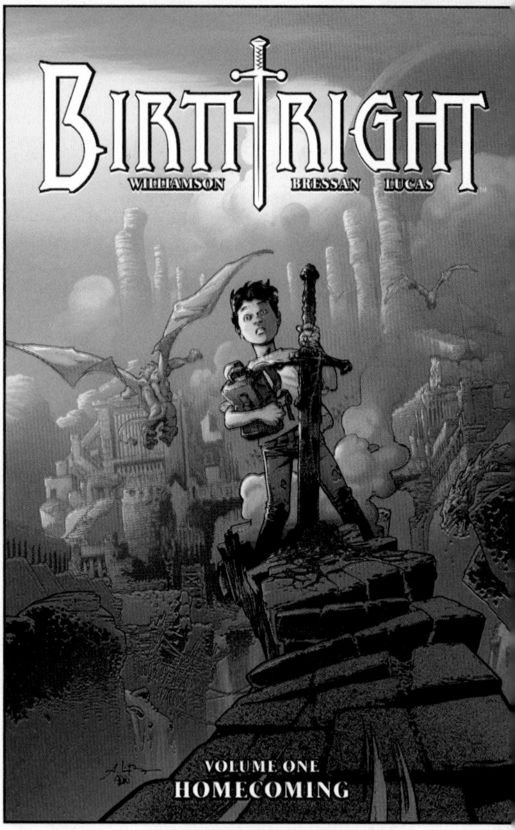

VOL. 1: HOMECOMING TP
ISBN: 978-1-63215-231-2
$9.99

VOL. 2: CALL TO ADVENTURE TP
ISBN: 978-1-63215-446-0
$12.99

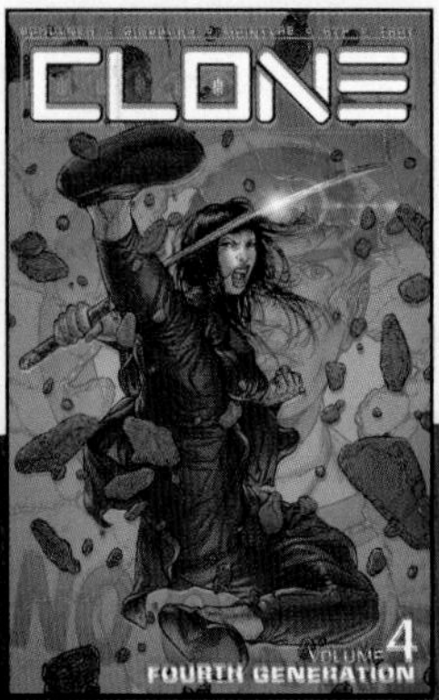

VOL. 1: FIRST GENERATION TP
ISBN: 978-1-60706-683-5
$12.99

VOL. 2: SECOND GENERATION TP
ISBN: 978-1-60706-830-3
$12.99

VOL. 3: THIRD GENERATION TP
ISBN: 978-1-60706-939-3
$12.99

VOL. 4: FOURTH GENERATION TP
ISBN: 978-1-63215-036-3
$12.99

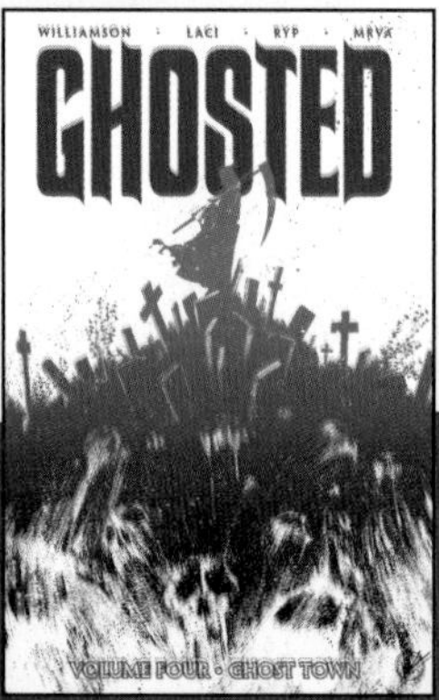

VOL. 1: HAUNTED HEIST TP
ISBN: 978-1-60706-836-5
$9.99

VOL. 2: BOOKS OF THE DEAD TP
ISBN: 978-1-63215-046-2
$12.99

VOL. 3: DEATH WISH TP
ISBN: 978-1-63215-051-6
$12.99

VOL. 4: GHOST TOWN TP
ISBN: 978-1-63215-317-3
$12.99

VOL. 1: UNDER THE KNIFE TP
ISBN: 978-1-60706-441-1
$12.99

VOL. 2: MAL PRACTICE TP
ISBN: 978-1-60706-693-4
$14.99

VOL. 1: FLORA & FAUNA TP
ISBN: 978-1-60706-982-9
$9.99

VOL. 2: AMPHIBIA & INSECTA TP
ISBN: 978-1-63215-052-3
$14.99

VOL. 3: CHIROPTERA & CARNIFORMAVES TP
ISBN: 978-1-63215-397-5
$14.99

BIRTHRIGHT™, CLONE™, GHOSTED™, MANIFEST DESTINY™, and WITCH DOCTOR™ © 2016 Skybound, LLC. OUTCAST BY KIRKMAN AND AZACETA™ © 2016 Robert Kirkman, LLC. Image Comics® and its logos are registered trademarks of Image Comics, Inc. Skybound and its logos are © and ™ of Skybound, LLC. All rights reserved.